# THE CH

by Stephanie Baudet

Illustrated by Gillian Marklew

ANGLIA *young* BOOKS

First published in 2004
by Anglia Young Books

Anglia Young Books is a division of
Mill Publishing
PO Box 120
Bangor
County Down
BT19 7BX

Illustrations by Gillian Marklew
Design by Adrian Baggett
Cover design by Andy Wilson

British Library Cataloguing-in-Publication Data

A catalogue record for this book is available from the British Library

ISBN 1 871173 96 5

Printed in Great Britain by Ashford Colour Press, Gosport, Hampshire

**Acknowledgements**

The author and publisher would like to thank Susan Fox, Keeper
of Collections at the Roman Baths in Bath, and Pastor Reg Coppard
for his Latin translation.

This story is set in the Roman town of Aquae Sulis, now called Bath. The events take place in the middle of the 4th century AD, at the time the Roman empire was converting to Christianity.

The Romans ruled England, Wales and parts of Scotland from AD 43 to AD 409.

# CHAPTER 1

The horse whinnied and reared up onto its hind legs and Julius jumped out of the way of the flailing hooves, still managing to hold on to the reins.

'Shhh,' he said, stroking its trembling neck, but still it skittered to one side in fright. This was one horse that could never be ridden by a soldier. No matter how hard they tried to train it to get used to the clashing of swords and shields and the shouts of men, it was as nervous as ever.

Julius gently pulled the animal's head down next to his own and spoke in a calm voice, just as his father had taught him. The sound of his voice had a soothing effect.

When he had finally coaxed the horse into its stable, rubbed it down and given it some feed, he knew he was late. His master would not be pleased. He washed in the trough and then ran all the way back through the city gate towards the baths.

Julius had been only a few days in Aquae Sulis. He and his mother and brother had come here all the way from Rome by boat with their master, Gaius Septimus Aquitanius, a recently retired army general. The army needed an endless supply of horses and here was an opportunity for the master to buy and train them. The Celts in Britannia bred very good horses.

Julius ran across the temple courtyard to the entrance of the baths and then paused to straighten his tunic and run his fingers through his hair. He had never been in these baths before, but they were famous throughout the empire. The naturally hot water that came up out of the earth was said to cure all sorts of ailments.

Entering the Great Bath he immediately felt hot in his tunic, especially after running all the way from the stables. He looked out over the steamy water and then at the stone columns rising up to form archways. Above these there were windows all the way round that let in shafts of slanted autumn sunlight. Higher still was the vaulted ceiling. The main baths in Rome were bigger still, but this building made Julius feel just as small.

From time to time the steam cleared and he could see the hazy figures of men bathing. Others

6

sat around on the steps. The hum of voices and the splash of someone leaping into the water echoed throughout the vast space.

Julius suddenly remembered his master would be waiting for him in the caldarium and went to find it.

His master was lying face down on a stone bench when Julius arrived. He raised his head a little to look at him. Wisps of short dark hair flecked with grey clung to his forehead, and his face shone with sweat.

'You are late, boy! I have no use for slaves who are not here when I want them.'

'I am so sorry, sir ...' began Julius. He was about to explain about the nervous horse but then thought better of it. The master would not listen to excuses. Instead, he quickly picked up the flask of oil and tipped a little into his hand, spilling some on the floor.

'What's the matter with you today, Julius?' shouted the master. 'First you are late and now you waste good oil by spilling it on the floor. I might regret that I ever had pity on you and bought you from the emperor, no matter who your father was. A boy, a woman and a child, what madness!'

'I am sorry, sir. Please forgive me. You will not regret it, sir.'

He carefully set the flask on the stone floor and then began to rub oil into his master's back. The warm oil mixed with pumice powder felt good beneath his fingers and he always enjoyed this job.

Yet it was true that his mind was on something else, and it was not the nervous horse. His little brother Benetus was ill. He had a fever and sore throat and had been sick twice during the night. Julius remembered how worried their mother had looked when he left that morning.

He picked up the strigil and began to scrape the oil and sweat off his master's skin. It was so hot and humid that sweat was soon trickling down his own back and making his tunic stick to him. At last he was finished and his master grunted and got up from the bench. Now he would plunge into the cold bath before meeting friends to discuss business and swim in the main pool.

Julius wiped up the spilt oil. His next task was to find some odd-jobs to do in the baths. There was always the chance of earning a little money from these jobs if he did them well. Money that he hoped would one day buy his freedom and that of his mother and brother.

That was once the dream of his father, Octavian, who had been a charioteer for the Green team in the Circus Maximus in Rome. His father had shown great skill, which could have earned freedom for himself and his family, but driving a chariot was very dangerous and a year ago he had been killed during a race.

Gaius Septimus Aquitanius had been a great admirer of Octavian, and after his death had bought Julius and his family from the emperor, who owned all four teams, the Greens, the Reds, the Blues and the Whites. Gaius could see that Julius showed signs of being good with horses and, even at eleven, had already learnt many skills from his father. Their mother was the mistress's personal slave and, one day, Benetus would also do his share of work.

Julius collected a pile of towels to take to the laundry. From the exercise room two men grunted with the effort of lifting weights, and from somewhere else a shriek of pain made Julius shudder. He knew that sound well enough, as men were plucked clean of body hair by the hair pluckers.

Julius's tasks earned him two maiorinae that day. He tucked the bronze coins into his tunic, ready to go into the clay pot with the rest of his savings. Then he remembered that there was a sacred spring in Aquae Sulis, and a statue of the goddess Minerva, although here she was called Sulis Minerva. He would offer one of the coins to her instead, and pray that she might make his brother well.

Julius ran from the baths to the temple courtyard. When he got there, he stood and looked up the steep steps to the temple's entrance, surrounded by four great columns. Inside stood the gilded bronze statue, though no one but priests were allowed to enter and see it.

With a pang of guilt he remembered that because his master was now a Christian, he was too. Yet he did not feel like one. How could you change your beliefs so quickly? He thought back to the small shrine his father had made in their living quarters in Rome. His family had prayed to the gods each day. Now he must learn about this new religion.

In the temple courtyard there were soothsayers, who offered to tell people's fortunes,

11

as well as scribes, with styluses and small lead squares, ready to write curses or prayers to be thrown into the sacred spring.

Julius could write well enough, so he bought a square of lead with one of his coins and borrowed a stylus. Then he sat on the paved ground and leaned against a stone altar. The smell of incense from the top of the altar drifted down and filled his nostrils. He began to write in the soft lead. Writing backwards made a prayer even more powerful so it took some time. At last he had finished and he read it through carefully.

*.evah I lla tub elttil*
*yrev si tI .aniroiam eno*
*fo tfig a uoy gnirb I*
*.suteneB ,rehtorb elttil*
*ym fo efil eht evas esaelP*
*.avreniM suliS taerg O*

Then he folded the square of lead and stood up. Facing the temple, Julius closed his eyes tightly. 'O great goddess,' he prayed silently. 'Please make Benetus well again.'

He turned and ran in through the entrance to the sacred spring itself. Reaching into his tunic, Julius grasped the other coin and flung it, with the folded lead square, into the round, steaming pool. Now he must get back to the baths. His master would be looking for him, and although he was not a cruel man, to be late again would risk a harsh punishment.

When he returned to the baths, Julius saw groups of men gathered in the alcoves around the main pool. In one of the alcoves he expected to find his master, talking with fellow traders. Some men came to gamble a little on a game of knucklebones or listen to philosophers, but not Gaius Septimus Aquitanius. He regarded such things as a waste of time and used his daily visits to the baths to make deals and discuss prices.

As Julius approached an alcove he heard his master's name spoken. He stopped to listen from behind a pillar, holding his breath. The speaker was talking quietly, but he had a deep, rough voice. Julius could not hear well above the noise of the baths, but he caught the words 'take his daughter' and 'pay'. He craned his head forward a little round the pillar.

'I shall enjoy seeing him suffer,' the man with the rough voice was saying. 'He made us suffer often enough.'

There was a harsh laugh from someone else.

'And we shall have enough money to pay off our debts and some to spare for the games.'

What was it all about? He could well imagine the master making someone suffer, but only if they had done wrong. Julius knew he was a fair man. And what was this about money and the master's daughter? Olivia was only eight years old and she and her brother Flavius were Julius's friends.

He leaned in further. Now he could see a hand, its fingers splayed out on the stone step. On the third finger was a gold ring set with a clear purple gemstone.

Julius was so intent on the ring that he was almost too slow to react when one of the men scrambled to his feet and stepped out from the alcove. For one moment Julius glimpsed his shadowy face, but then he fled, not daring to look back.

He found his master in the changing room and helped to dry him with a towel. 'May I speak to you, sir?' he asked, while he unfolded the master's toga. 'It is a matter of great importance.'

'Speak then,' said the master without looking at him.

'I overheard your name, sir,' Julius said. 'In the baths ... they said ... they said ...'

'Hurry up with that toga,' snapped the master. 'What are you gabbling on about?'

Julius draped the toga over his master's left shoulder and under his right arm. 'They talked about Olivia ... well, not her name, but ... and making you suffer. I think they're planning to kidnap her.'

The master glared at him. 'What nonsense is this? No one would dare! They'd get no money from me!' He took the edge of the toga from Julius and threw it over his shoulder with a flourish, tucking it into the umbilicus around his waist. Then he strode out of the door.

As Julius picked up the towel something caught his eye. On the stone bench was a neat pile of clothes, and on top a brooch for pinning a man's cloak. It was gold and in the centre a purple gemstone gleamed. It was the same design as the ring he had seen! They must belong to the same person. But who was he?

# CHAPTER 2

That afternoon, during the ninth hour of the day, Julius went to eat his meal and see Benetus. In their room next to the kitchen he bent over his young brother, lying in bed by the window. A rash had sprung up on his face and neck and the boy's eyes were closed.

Julius could feel the heat coming from his brother's fevered body and went to fetch a cloth soaked in cool water. Then he gently placed it across the boy's forehead.

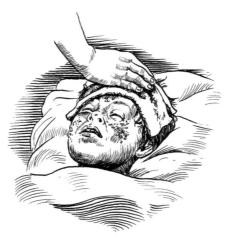

Benetus stirred and opened his eyes. They were pale and tired and lacked their usual mischievous sparkle. He opened his mouth as if to say something, but then just shook his head slightly.

'He cannot speak,' said their mother, softly, as she stroked her youngest son's face. 'His throat is very sore.'

Julius felt the worry sink in him like a heavy stone as he and his mother ate their meal of leftovers from the household. Neither of them felt much like eating or talking. His mother picked at her food, her face pale and drawn. She shivered and pulled at her woollen cloak, clasping it to her.

'If only we were still in Rome. I hear the winters are so cold here in Britannia. I feel a chill in the air already. No wonder Benetus is ill.'

Julius thought of Olivia. At any other time he would have told his mother what he had overheard in the baths, but at this moment she cared for no one's child except her own.

'Eat something, mother,' he said, seeing her pushing her food around the plate. 'I prayed to Sulis Minerva today and offered her a gift of money. Perhaps she will use her great power to make Benetus better.'

His mother looked up and smiled at him. 'You are a good boy, Julius, but you must forget about the old gods. We are Christians now, like our master. There is just one God. Mikalis has taught you, has he not?'

Julius nodded. Mikalis was the family's tutor, also a slave but an educated Greek. Each morning for two hours he taught Julius, Flavius and Olivia reading and writing and a little philosophy.

By next morning Benetus was worse and the doctor was sent for. He examined the boy and left some medicine, shaking his head.

Julius missed his lessons with the tutor to look after his brother while their mother helped to dress the mistress, Bella Augustina Aquitanius. The mistress was very particular about her clothes. Julius's mother had had to learn quickly how to please her.

Julius was so absorbed in his task of caring for Benetus that he almost forgot about the men in the baths, and even when it did cross his mind, he wondered if he had imagined it. But during the third hour of the day there was a commotion in the courtyard outside. When he went to see what was happening he was met by Flavius, who was trying to hold back his tears. For a moment he could not speak, and then the confident young Roman seemed to crumple before Julius's eyes.

'It's Olivia,' he said in a broken voice. 'She has disappeared. She was playing her lyre in the courtyard but now she has gone and it lies broken on the ground. Father sent me to find you. He says you know who has taken her.'

Minutes later, Julius stood before the master, who glowered at him from under heavy brows.

'Who are these men who have taken my daughter?' he roared.

'I don't know, sir,' said Julius. 'I did not see them. I only know that one of them had a rough voice and one had a signet ring.' He described the ring and the matching brooch. 'They spoke of making you suffer as you made them suffer.'

The master waved his hand in dismissal. 'I never made anyone suffer who did not deserve it,' he said. 'And what good is a voice and a ring? Are we to listen to every man in Aquae Sulis and demand to look at his hand?'

Julius did not know how to answer the master, so he stared at the ground.

A little later, as he set off to fetch water from the well, Julius watched a party of men leave to search the city. His own mother was comforting the mistress and behind him, in their small room, he could hear Benetus whimpering.

He turned to go back to his brother, but someone grasped his arm. It was Flavius.

'How can you not have seen them?' he demanded, shaking with rage and pulling at Julius's tunic. 'Why did you not tell my father? It was your duty.'

'I did tell him,' said Julius, quietly. 'But he would not listen.'

'Then you should have made him listen,' shouted Flavius. 'And you should have looked at these men so that you would remember them again. You are only a slave, your own safety means nothing.'

Julius had a sharp retort on his lips, but thought better of it. Although Flavius was his friend, he was also the master's son, and far superior to him. He must not answer him back.

'I'm sorry, Flavius. You are right. I only thought of my own safety.' He turned back to go to Benetus, but Flavius pulled harder on his tunic.

21

'No! You will not go back to your brother. I am sorry he is ill, but my sister must come first. We shall go into the forum and the baths and see if you can recognise this man.'

'But ...' Julius looked briefly back towards Benetus, then he nodded and followed Flavius.

◆     ◆     ◆

Something was going on in the forum. A crowd had gathered in front of the steps of the basilica. On the steps stood a man in a blue toga, a Roman.

'Who is he?' asked Julius, pausing to listen.

'He is a Christian preacher,' said Flavius.
'How can you not know? We should all pray to the
one God, now, and not the pagan idols. My father
has heard that the Roman authorities have taken
down some of the statues of pagan gods in parts
of the empire.'

Julius listened with dismay. He hoped that
the authorities would leave Sulis Minerva's statue
alone. He had never seen the statue, but he could
imagine what she looked like: life-size, golden and
beautiful, and very wise.

The boys walked through the forum. All at
once the preacher put his hands together with his
fingers pointing to the sky, and a hush fell on the
crowd.

'Our Father, who art in heaven …' he began.

'That's a prayer, isn't it?' whispered Julius.

'Of course it is,' said Flavius, a little irritably.
'We said it this morning after asking God for the
safe return of Olivia. Come on, we are wasting
time. The men will not be in this crowd. Let us go
to the baths.'

They went into the public baths, looking and
listening in every room and inspecting all the

clothes in the changing room. They ran up and down the narrow streets of the city, past shops and temples, but Julius did not hear the voice of the man nor see anyone wearing a gold brooch with a purple gemstone in the centre.

Julius and Flavius walked back to the villa. The master and his men had had no luck either. They had scoured the city and questioned many people, but had found no clues. Tomorrow they would search the farms outside the city.

Night came early as heavy clouds gathered and a cold, misty rain began to fall, which gathered in puddles on the paved roads. The noises of the city ceased as shops closed and people returned home to shut their doors against the weather.

It was late when Julius finally closed the door to his room. He crept over to Benetus and snuggled in beside the shivering boy. The sound of rain dripping off the roof only added to the gloom that had hung over the household all day.

# CHAPTER 3

It was Julius who found the ransom demand. He was in the kitchen, preparing the breakfast of bread, cheese and olives to take up to the master and his wife, when there was a sharp rap on the street door.

He opened the door. No one was there, but lying on the ground was a pair of wax tablets tied together with thin strips of leather. Beside the tablets was one of Olivia's enamel brooches, which she used to pin on her shawl. Julius picked them up. The brooch was silver with an inlaid enamel design in rich purple and green. It must have been the one she was wearing when she was kidnapped. Poor Olivia, Julius thought. How frightened she must be.

He liked the master's daughter. She was always kind to him and even stood up for him sometimes when Flavius made him feel small. She was a quiet girl, rather timid, but Julius hoped she would be strong and brave. He closed his hand over the brooch and then took a closer look at the wax tablets. The leather strips were not sealed. Julius knew he should take them straight to his master, but instead he undid the leather ties and opened the wooden tablets like a small book.

'*Habemus filiam tuam,*' he read. 'We have your daughter.' He read on. One hundred solidi! To be paid by the eleventh hour to get Olivia back!

Quickly tying the tablets together again, Julius ran up the stairs to his master's bedroom. He stopped outside the door, took a deep breath, and knocked before entering.

Gaius Septimus Aquitanius sat up as Julius entered. He frowned as he saw the wax tablets and a worried look came into his eyes as he realised what they were. They had been expecting it. Without a word, he stretched out his hand and took the tablets from Julius.

'One hundred solidi!' he exclaimed, shaking his head. 'How can I raise so much money?'

He fell back onto the pillow and the wax tablets clattered from his hand onto the floor. Julius had never seen the master like this before. His strong face, which usually showed authority, was slack and pale and his dark eyes stared blankly.

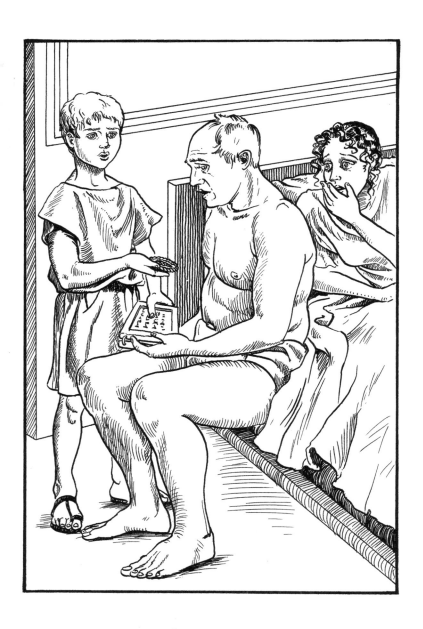

'They also left this, sir,' Julius said, placing the brooch on the table beside the bed. Then he crept from the room and went back to the kitchen, even though he doubted the family would be eating breakfast this morning.

Later, when Julius went up to the master's bedroom to shave him, the food brought up earlier had not been touched. The master was sitting on a chair beside his bed, staring down at the small silver brooch in his hand. In silence Julius draped a towel round his neck and gently raised the man's face to apply the oil and begin to shave. His master's cheeks were wet with tears.

Benetus's condition had not improved. Julius made his mother eat some bread and gave his brother a little water, which he had fetched from the spring. He watched with satisfaction as the boy swallowed it, and then gently wiped his lips with a cloth.

Instead of going to the stables that morning Julius stayed at the villa. Around the fourth hour he picked up a wooden bucket to go and fetch more water from the well, but Flavius stopped him as he left the house.

'We have to find these men,' said Flavius. 'You

must remember *exactly* what they said.'

Julius remembered the man's deep, rough voice. He would recognise it if he heard it again. He put the bucket down on the ground. They were outside the house and the street was busy and noisy. A mule brayed as it passed, its hooves clattering. A dog barked. Shopkeepers shouted their wares, and somewhere a small child cried.

But Julius heard none of it as he tried to remember what he had heard in the baths two days ago.

'I only caught a few words ...' he began, slowly. 'They spoke of seeing your father suffer as he had made them suffer. They said they could pay off their debts and have more for the games.'

'The games!' exclaimed Flavius. 'That's it! Come on!'

'But ...' Julius looked down at the bucket.

'Never mind that,' said Flavius. 'Can you not see? These men are gamblers and put money on the gladiator fights. We must go to the amphitheatre. There you may hear that voice again.'

# CHAPTER 4

'You've forgotten something,' said Julius, looking down at his simple tunic. 'Slaves are not allowed to watch the gladiator fights.'

'We'll soon make you into a Roman citizen,' declared Flavius, turning back into the house.

He soon returned with one of his own tunics and two white togas with a purple edge – the sign that they were worn by children.

Julius quickly put on the tunic and then the unfamiliar toga, draping the semicircle of cloth first over his left shoulder and passing the other end of it under his right arm and over his left shoulder again. It felt strange. How many times had he dreamed of being a freedman and a Roman citizen, entitled to wear a toga and to add his father's name to his own?

As he finished tucking in his toga, he noticed how excited Flavius looked. His eyes danced, and he kept hopping from one foot to the other.

Julius hoped that his friend would not be

disappointed. It seemed unlikely that he would hear and recognise a single voice from a crowd, but he said nothing.

Flavius's father was already out searching the surrounding farms for Olivia while the mistress tried to go calmly about her usual tasks, as all good Roman wives were expected to do. But she was red-eyed from crying and a sleepless night. Julius had heard that from his own mother.

Bella Augustina Aquitanius was all for scraping up the ransom money, but her husband indignantly refused. He did not love his daughter any the less, Julius knew, he was just outraged that anyone should make such demands. After the shock of receiving the ransom note his mood had changed. He had shouted at Julius for his clothes, and he seemed more determined than ever to catch the kidnappers. Perhaps as the eleventh hour approached he might change his mind.

◆      ◆      ◆

After asking the way, the two boys found the amphitheatre on the outskirts of the city. The street outside was quiet, since the games had already started, but they could hear the shouts of the spectators inside, sometimes cheering, sometimes booing.

The ticket seller had left his place at the entrance to the amphitheatre and was standing some way inside so he could watch the events. The two boys crept in and skirted round the outer walkway, going in by the next entrance.

The arena buzzed with excitement. A fight had just finished, and the spectators restlessly moved about, the men talking with their neighbours, calling out bets and watching impatiently for the next show to start. The sky was clear, but a cool autumn breeze lifted a scattering of fallen leaves in the centre of the arena and whirled them around.

Julius and Flavius climbed halfway up the sloping tiers of wooden seating and sat down. It was no use listening for the man's voice in all the noise. Better to wait until the contest started and the keener of the spectators began shouting.

'Who is fighting today?' asked Julius. He had never taken much interest in fighting contests before, although he knew that gladiators were slaves, like himself, or condemned convicts.

'The great Romulus,' said Flavius. 'He's a retiarius, fighting with just a net and trident. His opponent is Victian who has just arrived from

Rome. I heard his name on everyone's lips there. He is a secutor, who uses a sword and a shield. He daringly wears a purple plume in his helmet to mock tradition, but our great Emperor Constantine has no interest in the sport. He has outlawed it, although it is difficult to ban something so popular with the people.'

A hush fell over the whole arena and then a cheer went up as the two gladiators strode out from opposite sides. They held only wooden weapons for the warm-up and immediately began sparring, to the amusement of the crowd. Soon came the serious fighting. A fight to the death. Julius knew that much. He also knew that it was an honourable way to die. Slaves and condemned men were technically dead already, and did not exist in the eyes of many Roman citizens. Here was their chance to be somebody, and if they were good there was a slim possibility that they could win their freedom.

The fight began and Julius could see that the two gladiators were well matched. He found that he was riveted to the circle of ground and the fighting men, the grunts as they thrust forward with their weapons, the clash of trident on shield, or the whip of the weighted net capturing the sword. The crowd roared at the first sight of blood.

As the tension mounted, Julius forced himself to focus his attention and listen to the men in the crowd. He also decided that it was no good sitting in one place. They needed to move around. He nudged Flavius.

As they stood up so did the crowd. The noise was deafening. When things settled down, the boys walked along an empty row, still watching the fight. Romulus's body glistened with sweat, as well as blood from a gashed arm. He was circling Victian, his trident held high with one hand, swinging his net menacingly with the other hand. Victian's face was covered by his helmet, so no one could see whether he was weakening or not. The helmet and the shield were heavy and he could not move as fast as Romulus, but he had more protection. Both men wore brief covering on the lower half of their bodies and sandals on their feet, but Victian also wore a metal breast plate.

Men were on their feet now, shouting and waving their fists. Julius listened as they passed. How could he ever hear one voice from all these? Flavius kept looking at him questioningly, but each

time he shook his head.

'Look!' said Flavius, pointing. 'You see that soldier in uniform? His name is Cassius Pontius Agrippa. He is a centurion from Isca, who has come here to take the waters for his health. It is he who will decide the fate of the loser today.'

Just then another roar went up and the boys looked into the arena. Romulus was standing over Victian, his trident at the other gladiator's throat.

'Let him go!' shouted someone nearby, and others took up the same chant.

Suddenly, they heard another voice. It was low and rough and full of menace.

'Kill him!'

Julius looked at Flavius and nodded excitedly. This was the man. He was sure!

'Kill him!' The one voice was lost as others joined in.

But Julius did not know where the first voice had come from.

Nothing could be done until Victian's fate had been decided. All eyes were on the centurion. Would he be spared? The centurion looked around at the crowd. Then he raised a white handkerchief. Victian was to be spared to fight another day.

The crowd began to leave their seats and move towards the exits. Julius and Flavius darted among them, searching for the ring or the brooch. Many were wearing warm cloaks covering their togas as clouds gathered overhead.

Then the sun came out again and something flashed, catching Julius's eye. About ten paces to their left he could see a man with a brown cloak, which was held in place by a heavy gold brooch. In the centre of the brooch a stone flashed purple as its facets caught the sun. The man was heavily built, with a large, square face and a squashed nose, like a boxer's.

'You see?' said Julius, excitedly.

'We will follow him when he leaves,' whispered Flavius.

The man in the brown cloak was clearly not pleased. He had won, but it had not been a fight to the death as he had wished. His face was creased with anger and his brows bunched in a scowl. He muttered something to the shorter, balding man beside him and they left the amphitheatre.

Flavius and Julius were not far behind.

# CHAPTER 5

Out in the street, the crowd began to thin as people went in different directions. It was not hard for Julius and Flavius to follow the man with the rough voice, since he was a little taller than average. His disappointment at not seeing the loser killed had left him, and his win had put him in a good mood. This mood was helped by the jug of wine he carried, from which he kept drinking and passing to his companion. The two men stopped at one of the many open-fronted shops along the street and had their jug refilled. They climbed aboard a cart pulled by a grey mare, and one of them tossed a coin to the slave who had been looking after it.

Flavius looked at Julius in dismay. 'They must live outside the city,' he said, as the two boys watched from behind a pillar. 'How can we follow a horse?'

'We must try,' said Julius. His father, Octavian, had had grey mares too, he remembered. Four matching greys. What beauties they had been! Such spirited horses, but they would do anything for his father. Time after time they had smoothly turned at the end of the stadium like one being, hardly losing any speed, and then roared down the straight again, tails and manes flying. Behind them, in his small golden chariot, Octavian had stood, legs apart, reins in one hand and whip in the other, his green cape flying behind, as the crowd urged him on.

'Julius!' hissed Flavius, tugging at his toga. 'Come on!'

It was fairly easy to follow the two men while they were inside the city wall. The roads were narrow and always busy, so their horse had to walk. The men also stopped at several shops to pick up food supplies and wine and load them onto the cart. But once through the city gates and on the open road they broke into a trot, although the horse seemed to be going at its own pace with very little direction from its driver, the man with the rough voice. From time to time he put down the reins to swig at the jug of wine.

'They are not used to driving horses,' panted Julius. 'Usually it is done by a slave.'

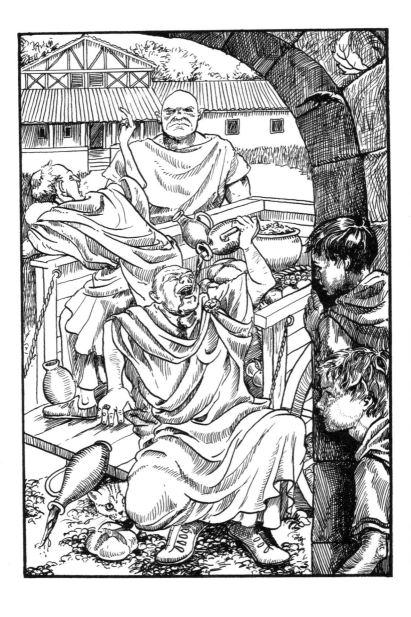

'Maybe their slaves have other duties at present,' said Flavius. 'Like holding my sister captive.'

Julius looked at his friend. There was a mixture of excitement and worry in his voice.

Some two miles from the city the horse turned in through a gateway and slowed to a walk, knowing it was home. Julius and Flavius had followed from a distance and now watched from behind a wall as the two men slithered down from the wagon and tottered unsteadily towards the door of the farmhouse.

'Brutus!' yelled the balding man.

A huge man appeared from one of the outbuildings. He wore a simple brown tunic and his arms and legs bulged with muscles. He was the biggest man Julius had ever seen.

A small cat rubbed against the man's ankles and he swiftly kicked out at it, sending it flying through the air with a yowl. Julius had not realised there were cats in Britannia, too. Maybe the Romans had brought them over to kill the rats and mice in their grain stores. Well, if Olivia was here .... Julius smiled inwardly, remembering how often they had teased Olivia about her fear of cats.

'Is our hostage safe?' asked the man with the rough voice. The slave nodded.

'Then unload the wagon!'

He put his arm around the shoulders of the balding man. 'Come, brother,' he said. 'We have enough wine to sink a ship, and more than enough reason to celebrate. We shall soon be rich, and we shall see Gaius grovel!' The two men walked inside the farmhouse. The door slammed shut behind them.

'Olivia must be here somewhere,' said Flavius, watching the cat pick itself up and wander into the grain store. 'But how can we possibly rescue her with that huge slave around?'

His look of despair was shared by Julius. If Flavius did not know what to do, then he would have to think of something – and quickly.

At that moment they heard a muffled scream from one of the outbuildings.

# CHAPTER 6

'She *is* here!' said Flavius. 'They must be holding her in the grain store – with the cat!'

They watched as Brutus unloaded the stores from the wagon and took them into a small building next to the house. From somewhere inside Julius heard a dog bark. So they had hunting dogs too! The chances of rescuing Olivia were getting smaller and smaller. Julius looked up at the sun. It was about the ninth hour already. Soon the ransom must be paid or ... or what? He knew that they had to distract Brutus before he unhitched the horse.

'Flavius, you must get to Olivia while that slave is busy unloading,' he whispered. 'I shall distract his attention and when I shout you must both come out running and jump onto the wagon.'

Flavius nodded and Julius smiled inwardly at the idea of his friend taking orders from him, a slave.

When Brutus disappeared into the store

room, Flavius darted in through the gate and made for the nearest building, the stables, hiding behind the wooden pillars that divided the horses' stalls. From there he edged his way round the stone walls of the grain store to its wooden door.

Julius watched him go. He still had no clear idea of what he was going to do. His toga had slipped off his left shoulder and he swept it back over and tucked it in again. As he was adjusting his unfamiliar clothing, the idea came to him.

With no time to feel nervous, Julius marched into the courtyard just as Brutus was emerging from the store. The big man stopped in surprise.

'Slave!' cried Julius. 'Fetch water! Quickly! My father has been taken ill in his carriage, some two hundred paces from here. We dare not continue until he has rested and had a drink.'

Julius's voice held much more authority than he felt, but he knew he had to sound convincing or all would be lost.

Brutus glanced towards the grain store. 'But I ...'

Julius stamped his foot. 'Do not answer me back! My father is Julius Gaius Octavian, and he is going to Aquae Sulis on behalf of the emperor.

Tend to him at once or he will have you executed!'

Brutus still did not move. He looked calmly back at Julius. There was a questioning look in his eyes. Julius held the huge man's gaze although he was quaking inside. Could Brutus recognise another slave? Was there some tell-tale sign?

At last, Brutus seemed to come to a decision. After glancing behind him at the farmhouse, he grabbed a flask and ran to fill it at the water trough. Julius pointed along the road away from the city and made to go with him, but as soon as he was out of sight, Julius called softly to Flavius. At the same time he leapt aboard the wagon, grabbed the reins, and expertly turned the surprised horse around.

There was no sound from inside the grain store and Julius looked anxiously at the farmhouse door. He could hear the dog barking. At any moment the two men might appear. And it was not going to take Brutus long to find out that there was no carriage.

His heart thudded in his chest and the horse skittered around nervously, its hooves clattering on the stone paving.

Then they appeared, Flavius and Olivia. She looked pale and had been crying, but Flavius lifted her aboard and swung up himself as Julius shook the reins. The wagon leapt forward.

They all held on tightly as the grey mare flew through the gates and turned right onto the Fosse Way, heading back to the city. Behind came shouts and the barking of dogs, which had reached a frenzied pitch. Julius knew they had been let out.

He looked round quickly. Brutus was running past the gate just as three dogs came out. For a moment the big man paused and the dogs leapt at him, mistaking him for the intruder, but he pushed them off with a stroke of his arm and together they gave chase to the wagon.

Julius shrieked at the horse, urging it on. He stood, like a true charioteer, feet apart, the wind streaming past his ears, his toga unwrapped and flying behind him. Today he was driving for the Whites, since his toga was white. What would his father have said about that! Despite the danger they were in he grinned and flapped the reins so that they clipped the horse's glistening sides.

Brutus was a powerful runner despite his size, and while the horse was adjusting its stride he was almost upon them, reaching out to grasp the end of the wagon. Olivia gave a little scream as his fingers touched and almost curled over the wooden

frame. Julius saw this as he glanced round again, and urged the horse forward.

But just when it looked as if they were going to make it, Julius felt a violent bump underneath the wagon. One of the wheels had hit a rock in the middle of the road! He could feel the vehicle begin to wobble from side to side, and no matter how hard he shouted at the grey mare and flicked the reins, he knew they had lost speed. The poor horse ran as fast as it could, but the wagon swayed all over the road and the children felt it tip dangerously over to one side.

And then Brutus was there. He was now running alongside the wagon and Julius could hear his deep breaths above the sounds of the horse and the juddering vehicle. Brutus had his hand on the side of the wagon, and seemed to be trying to slow it down. Julius heard the big man grunt with effort – any second now he would dig his heels into the road and pull the cart to a standstill. It would all be over.

Just then, however, one of the excited dogs also caught up with them. It crashed straight into Brutus, who lost his grip on the wagon and then his balance. There was a yelp from the dog, who just managed to scuttle out of the way as the enormous slave crashed to the ground.

'Keep going!' screamed Flavius to Julius. 'We can still make it!' Julius shook the reins as hard as he could. The wagon picked up speed again, although the loose wheel made it tremble so hard that Olivia nearly fell out. Flavius made her sit between his legs as he held on to the wooden sides with both hands.

Julius looked over his shoulder. Brutus and the dogs were a speck in the distance. The horse turned a corner and then he could not see anything behind them at all.

But his problems were not over. The wagon's shaking was getting worse and worse. Suddenly, with no sound at all, the damaged wheel broke loose and spun off into the ditch. With a crack, one of the shafts of the wagon snapped and fell out of the harness. The vehicle tipped over and the children felt everything turn upside-down as they were flung out into the road.

But Julius was on his feet in an instant, grabbing the horse's harness.

'Quickly! Onto the horse!'

He leapt upon the horse's back, calling to

Flavius, who lifted his sister aboard and scrambled up himself. He could ride almost as well as Julius and grasped Olivia round the waist, clamping his own knees against the horse.

'Hold on!' shouted Julius, and with a clatter of hooves they were off again. He glanced at a milestone by the side of the road. *Aquae Sulis M P 1*. One mile to the city.

The road was still wet from the previous night's rain and sometimes the horse slithered on a slippery paving stone. Then Julius felt Olivia's hands tighten around his waist and heard her gasp with fear. Once he placed his hand over hers and squeezed it reassuringly, and once he looked back to see if they were still being followed.

It was more than Brutus's life was worth to let them escape and he felt sorry for the big man.

They slowed down as they entered the city gates. Brutus would not catch them now. They had done it!

But before any of them had a chance to breathe a sigh of relief or congratulate themselves, they noticed that something strange was going on. People were running and shouting. Something was happening near the baths.

# CHAPTER 7

Julius, Flavius and Olivia dismounted. Julius could see excited expressions on people's faces. He had the impression that everyone was waiting for something to happen.

The horse had been nervous enough before but now, with the people and the noise, it pranced around wildly, eyes staring and flecks of white foam appearing around its mouth.

'You take Olivia home,' Julius told Flavius. 'I'll see to the horse.' Here he was giving the orders again, but somehow he felt that he had earned the right. Flavius just nodded. Julius watched briefly as the two disappeared into the crowd and then he led the horse to a stable nearby and handed it over to a slave. If the kidnappers did not reclaim their horse and pay for its livery, he knew his master would. They could never have rescued Olivia without it.

The huge crowds now blocked his way so he was swept along to the temple courtyard. The same preacher from the day before was standing on the steps of the temple. Julius strained to hear what he was saying.

'God chose to send his son Jesus to live among us as an ordinary man,' the preacher said. 'Jesus sacrificed himself to pay for the sins of man. God gave us ten commandments, and the first one says *I am the Lord thy God, thou shalt have no other gods but me.*'

Suddenly the crowd parted as four horsemen galloped through. For a moment Julius thought it was the men from the farm. He saw the horses' gleaming brown flanks and smelled their sweat as they clattered past and came to a halt in front of the temple.

But as the men leapt to the ground, he noticed the familiar plumed helmet of a centurion with three legionaries standing next to him, their metal breast plates glinting in the sun. They ran up the steps and into the dark depths of the temple. A few minutes later the crowd gasped in awe as they saw the statue of Sulis Minerva for the first time. She appeared head first at the entrance, her golden body gleaming in the sunlight.

The soldiers dragged the statue to the edge of the steps, stood it up and then stepped back. For a moment it remained standing and then began to topple forward.

People standing nearby, including the preacher, fell back like a field of wheat bowed down by the wind.

The statue crashed onto the steps. Julius, unable to see over other people's heads, pushed through the stunned crowd until he could see the goddess lying in pieces, her head still intact except for a dent above her right eye. The helmet had come off her head and lay beside it on the ground.

Some people cheered as the soldiers swung onto their horses and galloped back through the crowd and out of the city.

Sulis Minerva was no more.

'Praise be to God!' shouted someone and several more took up the cry.

Julius stared at the head of the goddess, her calm, wise eyes looking up at the sky. He thought with dismay of the offering he had made to her for his brother's health. How could she have any power now?

As the crowd withdrew Julius took one last look at the golden head and then boldly climbed the steep steps and walked in through the four pillars to the forbidden temple. There he sat for some time, staring at the plinth where the goddess had stood.

Julius could not take in all that had happened that day. The gladiator fight, following the kidnappers to the farm, then rescuing Olivia and the chase back to the city with Brutus on their heels. And if that was not enough, now Sulis Minerva had been destroyed before his eyes.

At last, he emerged from the temple. The goddess's head had gone but her helmet was still there. Julius walked back home feeling very confused. He was glad that they had got Olivia home safely, but what about Benetus?

He pushed open the door of the courtyard.

The first person he saw was Olivia, who ran out and flung her arms around his waist. She was followed by the whole family and the rest of the slaves. Julius stopped, wondering what was happening. He looked into the faces of the master and his wife and could not believe the smiles of joy that were directed at him. Him, a slave! They were looking at him as an equal. The master stepped forward and patted him on the shoulder.

'You have done well, Julius,' he said. 'It is thanks to you that I have my daughter back. We have sent men to arrest the kidnappers.'

The mistress hugged Julius to her and Flavius jumped up and down trying to get everyone's attention.

'You should have seen him with the horse, father. He was *so* good! And then that slave Brutus came after us. He was HUGE. And he tripped over one of the dogs.' Flavius let out a peal of laughter. 'It was *so* funny!'

It seemed that everyone was talking and then

were suddenly silent. Julius saw that the master was looking beyond him, and he turned to see two men being dragged into the courtyard and thrown to the ground. They lay there staring up at the master. One of them spat at him.

'Curses on you and your family!' It was the man with the rough voice.

The master smiled, although there was no warmth in his face. 'I hoped I'd seen the last of you two when I threw you out of the army,' he said. 'Still causing trouble I see?'

'Trouble!' said the man with the rough voice. 'You'll see trouble one of these days. May you suffer just as you made us do, rotting in jail.'

Julius watched his master's face darken. 'You were in the army to serve your emperor and your country, and you did little of either. You brought shame to the legion with your gambling and drunkenness and deserved everything you got.' He nodded and the men were taken away.

As if they had never been interrupted, the master turned back to Julius.

'Your father would be proud of you, Julius,' he said. 'I give you your freedom and that of your mother and brother too. From this moment you are a freedman and a Roman citizen, but I would like you to stay and help me train the horses – for a wage, of course.'

Julius could not believe his ears. Him a freedman!

'So you can keep the toga,' put in Flavius. 'Now you are a Roman citizen you are allowed to wear it.'

Julius looked down at the toga, roughly thrown over his shoulder since the wild horse ride. There was another thing he could do now he was a Roman citizen – something much more important than wearing a toga. He could call himself Julius Gaius Octavian, after his master out of respect and after his father out of love.

Just then there was a movement at the kitchen door. Julius looked up and saw his mother coming out. Her back was straighter and she held her head high. Her face was smooth and soft. Julius met her eyes and held his breath as he waited for her to speak.

'The fever is gone,' she said, quietly. 'Your brother will live.'

'God has answered all our prayers,' said the mistress.

Julius felt his worries melt into the air. Olivia still clung to him and he ruffled her hair.

'I was so afraid of that creature,' she said. 'You saved me from him.'

'Brutus?' asked Julius. 'He didn't hurt you, did he?'

'She means the cat, of course,' said Flavius. 'The only Roman to be afraid of cats!' He made a purring noise and clawed his fingers.

Julius smiled. 'I have heard that some people have them for pets,' he said. 'Perhaps I shall get you one.' They all laughed when Olivia shrieked.

'Father is also giving you a little house to live in,' announced Flavius.

Julius looked at the man who had been his master. 'Thank you, sir,' he said. 'There is just one more thing I ask.'

'Name it,' the master replied.

'It is that Flavius should teach me the prayer that the preacher was saying in the forum yesterday.'

'I know it by heart,' said Flavius, proudly. 'It is called The Lord's Prayer.'

# EPILOGUE

The Roman city of Aquae Sulis, today known as Bath, lay on the Fosse Way, a military road linking Exeter and Lincoln. In the early days of the Roman rule of Britannia, this road was heavily fortified to protect the conquered land of south-east England from the Celts.

The warm spring in Aquae Sulis was already known to the local people, who were called the Dobunni. They believed its waters were sacred to their goddess Sulis, and that they had healing powers.

The Romans were fond of bathing, and all Roman towns had public baths, usually heated with great furnaces. The water gushing out of the ground at Aquae Sulis, however, was naturally hot. It was – and today still is – 46° Celsius (body temperature is 37° Celsius!). The public bathhouse in Aquae Sulis became well known throughout the Roman empire. People came to bathe and drink the water, which they believed could cure diseases.

When the Romans left Britannia in the early 5th century, the baths were abandoned and gradually fell into ruin. The water rose and flooded the site, covering it in black mud. It was not until the 18th century that parts of the baths were seen and recorded. They were put on display only in the late 19th century and the extent seen today was revealed only in the early 1980s.

The Romans worshipped many gods. When they arrived in Britannia they realised their gods had many things in common with the Celtic gods. Minerva was the Roman goddess of wisdom, healing and war. In Aquae Sulis the Romans merged her with the Celtic goddess Sulis to become Sulis Minerva.

The Romans made a gilded (gold-covered) bronze statue of Sulis Minerva, slightly larger than life-size, which they placed in a small temple in Aquae Sulis. Only priests could enter the temple, but next to it, in a separate building, was a sacred spring into which people could make offerings to the goddess. Like Julius in the story, people made offerings in the belief that Sulis Minerva would answer their prayers.

61

In 1727, Sulis Minerva's head was found in Bath's Stall Street by workmen digging a sewer. It had been buried a few metres from the goddess's temple. The head, which is now on display in the museum at the Roman Baths in Bath, shows signs of deliberate damage. There is a huge dent by the right eye and the neck looks as though it has been torn from its body. No one knows for certain who attacked the statue. Some people think it may have been tribes who opposed the Romans; other people think it may have been the Roman authorities themselves, destroying pagan symbols after Christianity began to spread throughout the Roman empire in the time of Emperor Constantine (c. 280–337).

Little is known about the city of Aquae Sulis. For the purposes of this story it is assumed that there was an amphitheatre, as there was in most Roman cities. It is an exciting thought that there may still be ruins of the Roman city underneath the present-day town of Bath, just waiting to be discovered.

# GLOSSARY

**basilica:** a Roman town hall.

**caldarium:** the hot room.

**centurion:** a Roman army officer.

**chariot racing:** a very popular sport in Roman times. Charioteers were either slaves or condemned prisoners. They could become superstars and earn their freedom if they were really good. They raced small two-wheeled chariots with a team of four horses around seven laps.

**Circus Maximus:** the main venue in Rome for chariot racing. The ruins can still be seen today.

**forum:** a public square, usually with the basilica on one side and other public buildings around. It was used for markets and public meetings.

**gladiators:** slaves or condemned criminals trained to fight animals or each other, usually to the death.

**hair pluckers:** people who removed body hair. The Romans preferred not to have any body hair except that on their heads.

**scribe:** a person who was paid to write for people who did not know how.

**solidus (plural solidi):** a gold coin weighing 4.5 grams.

**soothsayer:** a fortune-teller.

**strigil:** a metal instrument for scraping oil and dirt off skin.

**stylus:** a pointed iron pen for writing on wax tablets.

**Sulis Minerva:** the goddess of wisdom, healing and military power. The Romans thought that their goddess Minerva was very similar to the Celtic goddess Sulis. The statue in Aquae Sulis was made of gilded bronze. Only the head was ever found and is in the museum in Bath.

**toga:** an item of clothing worn by Roman men, made of a semicircular piece of material draped over and under the shoulders. Only the emperor could wear a purple one, but boys under 14 (as well as magistrates and senators) wore a white toga with purple edges.

**trident:** a three-pronged spear.

**umbilicus:** a woven belt around the waist into which the toga was tucked.

**wax tablet:** a wooden board spread with a layer of wax for writing on with a stylus.